Ladybird  Readers

# Topsy and Tim
# The Big Race

Series Editor: Sorrel Pitts
Text adapted by Coleen Degnan-Veness
Illustrated by Belinda Worsley

LADYBIRD BOOKS

UK | USA | Canada | Ireland | Australia
India | New Zealand | South Africa

Ladybird Books is part of the Penguin Random House group of companies
whose addresses can be found at global.penguinrandomhouse.com.
www.penguin.co.uk    www.puffin.co.uk    www.ladybird.com

First published 2016
001
Copyright © Jean and Gareth Adamson, 2016

The moral rights of the author and illustrator have been asserted.

Printed in China

A CIP catalogue record for this book is available from the British Library

ISBN: 978-0-241-25448-6

Ladybird Readers

# Topsy and Tim
# The Big Race

By Jean and Gareth Adamson

# Picture words

Topsy

Tim

Mommy

spoon

hoops

sacks

umbrella

dressing up

race

Topsy and her brother, Tim had the same birthday. They were twins. The twins liked running.

They always ran together. Sometimes Topsy came first and sometimes Tim came first. They did not like coming second!

It was sports day at school.

Mommy came to school with Topsy and Tim. She wanted to watch the twins run.

"Tim, I can run very fast," said Topsy. "I want to come first in all the sports day races."

"You cannot come first!" said Tim.

"Yes, I can!" said Topsy.

In the first sports day race Topsy and Tim ran fast but they did not come first.

They were not happy.

In the second race the children had to throw hoops.

"I can come first in this race," said Topsy.

"No, you cannot! But I can!" said Tim.

But Topsy and Tim were not good at hoops and they did not come first.

The twins were not happy.

The next race was the sack race.

Topsy and Tim were not good at the sack race. They did not come first and they were not happy.

The next race was the dressing-up race. The children had to wear big coats and hats. They had to open umbrellas.

Topsy and Tim liked dressing up but their umbrellas did not open. They did not come first and they were not happy.

The next race was
the egg and spoon
race. This race was
only for moms.

Topsy and Tim's
mommy ran very
fast with the egg
and spoon—and
she came first!

Topsy and Tim had to run together for the next race.

"We must come first," they said.

Topsy and Tim ran very fast—and they came first!

They were very happy!

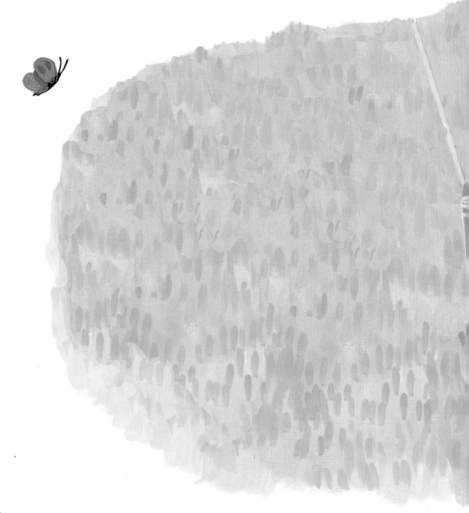

"You came first together!" said Mommy. And she was very happy, too!

# Activities

The key below describes the skills practiced in each activity.

Spelling and writing

Reading

Speaking

Critical thinking

Preparation for the Cambridge Young Learners Exams

**1** Look and read.
Put a ✓ or a ✗ in the box.  ○

**1**  This is Mommy.

**2**  This is Tim.

**3**  This is Topsy.

**4**  Topsy and Tim are twins. 

**5**  This is a race.

**2** **Look and read.**
**Write *yes* or *no*.**

Topsy and her brother, Tim had the same birthday. They were twins. The twins liked running.

They always ran together. Sometimes Topsy came first and sometimes Tim came first. They did not like coming second!

6                                              7

**1** Topsy and Tim have got the same birthday.                     _yes_

**2** Tim is Topsy's brother.

**3** The twins do not like running.

**4** The twins never run together.

**5** The twins do not like coming second in a race.

**3** Work with a friend.
Talk about the two pictures.
How are they different? 💬

a

In the first sports day race
Topsy and Tim ran fast but
they did not come first.

They were not happy.

12

b

Topsy and Tim ran very
fast—and they came first!

They were very happy!

26

27

**Example:**

In picture a, Topsy
is not happy.

In picture b,
Topsy is happy.

**4** **Look and read.**
**Write *yes* or *no*.**

1 Tim is not happy.  ........yes........

2 Mommy is talking
  to the twins.  ........................

3 The cat is in front
  of Mommy.  ........................

4 Topsy is happy.  ........................

**5** **Look at the picture. Look at the letters. Write the words.**

It was sports day at school.

Mommy came to school with Topsy and Tim. She wanted to watch the twins run.

**1** t s s p o r

**2** m m M o y

**3** s n w t i

**4** c e s r a

**1** It was s p o r t s day at school.

**2** _____ came to school with Topsy and Tim.

**3** Mommy wanted to watch the _____ .

**4** Topsy wanted to come first in all the sports day _____ .

35

**6** **Circle the correct word.**

**1** In the second race the children had to throw

   **a** bedroom    **( b hoops )**

**2** "I can come first in this race," said

   **a** Tim        **b** Topsy

**3** "No, you cannot!" said

   **a** Tim        **b** Topsy

**4** Topsy and Tim wanted to come

   **a** second     **b** first

**7** Look at the pictures. One picture
is different. How is it different?
Tell your teacher. ○

**1**

Picture a is different because
Topsy and Tim are fighting.

**2**

## 8 Write the correct words.

big  brown  blue  red  long  orange

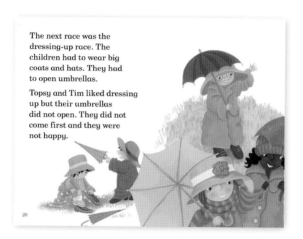

The next race was the dressing-up race. The children had to wear big coats and hats. They had to open umbrellas.

Topsy and Tim liked dressing up but their umbrellas did not open. They did not come first and they were not happy.

20

**1** Topsy has got ....big...., ...red... shoes.

**2** Tim has got a ........................,

........................ coat.

**3** Topsy is wearing a ........................,

........................ jacket.

**4** The boy with glasses is wearing a

........................, ........................ hat.

**9** **Ask and answer the questions with a friend.**

1 Did you dress up in your mommy and dad's clothes when you were little?

Yes, I did.

2 Do you like dressing up now?

3 What are your favorite clothes for dressing up?

4 Do you like dressing-up races?

**10** Look and read. Put a  or a **X** in the box. 📖 ❀ ❓

"Tim, I can run very fast," said Topsy. "I want to come first in all the sports day races."

"You cannot come first!" said Tim.

"Yes, I can!" said Topsy.

**1** Children like coming first in races.

**2** Twins have the same mommy and dad.

**3** Teachers help the children on sports day.

**4** Children wear long trousers and dresses on sports day.

**11** **Write Who, What, or Where.**

1 ___Who___ came first in the
egg and spoon race?

2 _____ did the moms carry
on their spoons?

3 _____ was the egg
and spoon race? Was it inside
or outside?

4 _____ came first in the
sack race?

5 _____ did the children
wear for the dressing-up race?

**12** **Ask and answer questions about the sack race with a friend.**

The next race was the sack race.

Topsy and Tim were not good at the sack race. They did not come first and they were not happy.

18

19

## Example:

> How many children were in the sack race?

> There were ten children in the sack race.

**13** **Read the text. Choose the correct words and write them on the lines.** 📖 ✏️ ⬡

| | | | |
|---|---|---|---|
| **1** | bad | easy | good |
| **2** | dressing up | sports day | hoops |
| **3** | come | coming | came |
| **4** | was | were | where |

Topsy was not ¹ ___good___

at hoops. And Tim was not good at

² _____ . They did not

³ _____ first. The twins

⁴ _____ not happy.

**14** Draw a picture of you and a friend in a race at sports day.

**15** **Talk about your picture with a friend.**

1

> Which sport are you doing?

> The sport I am doing is running.

2 Is that your favorite sport? Why?

3 Do you enjoy sports day at school?

4 Which races are you good at?

**16** **Look at the pictures.**
**Tell the story to your teacher.** 🗨

**Example:**

*Topsy and Tim liked running . . .*

**17** **Read the text. Choose a word from the box. Write the correct word next to numbers 1—5.**

In the first sports day race Topsy and Tim ran fast but they did not come first.

They were not happy.

come    first    happy    ran

In the ¹ _first_ sports day race,

Topsy and Tim ran fast but they did

not ² _____ first. They were not

³ _____ . Their friends ⁴ _____

fast.

# Level 2

Level 2

**The Gingerbread Man**

978–0–241–25442–4 ☐

Level 2

**Sly Fox and Red Hen**

978–0–241–25443–1 ☐

Level 2

**The Monster Next Door**

978–0–241–25444–8 ☐

Level 2

**Wild Animals**

978–0–241–25445–5 ☐

Level 2

**Little Red Riding Hood**

978–0–241–25446–2 ☐

Level 2

**Dinosaurs**

978–0–241–25447–9 ☐

Level 2

**Topsy and Tim The Big Race**

978–0–241–25448–6 ☐

Level 2

**Peter Rabbit Goes to the Treehouse**

978–0–241–25449–3 ☐

Level 2

**Sports Day**

978–0–241–26222–1 ☐

Level 2

**Going on a Picnic**

978–0–241–26221–4 ☐

## Now you're ready for Level 3!

**Notes**
CEFR levels are based on guidelines set out in the Council of Europe's European Framework. Cambridge Young Learners English (YLE) Exams give a reliable indication of a child's progression in learning English.